Seduced

One Handed Reads
Book 3

Dee Lish

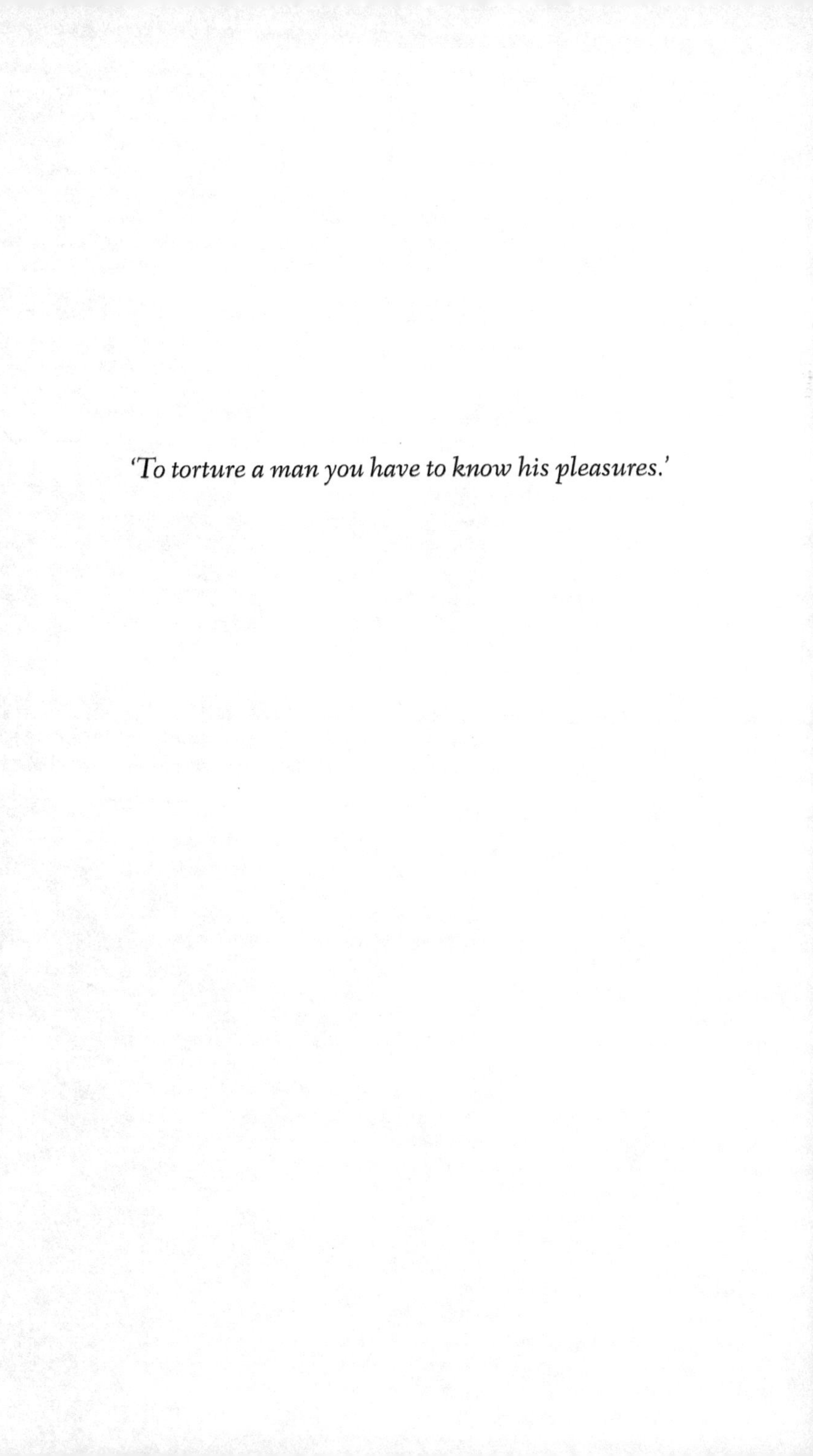

'To torture a man you have to know his pleasures.'

Chapter One

It doesn't normally happen this way, but when I see him, the attraction is something I just can't ignore. There is just something about him that lures me to him when I see him across the hotel bar. It doesn't take long before we're in the lift, heading for his room. The temptation is too much, and as soon as the lift doors close, I pounce, forcing him up against the wall of the elevator car, pushing his hands above his head and crushing my lips to his. His fingers link with mine as I hold his hands above his head, grinding my body against his as my tongue hungrily fucks his mouth. He growls deep in his chest and pushes back against me, forming his body to mine, letting me feel his length against my stomach, inviting me for more.

When the lift dings, announcing we have arrived at his floor, I push myself off him, keeping one hand locked with his, and pull him behind me. "Room number?" I demand seductively.

"Three-oh-nine," he replies, and I pull him in the direction of his room.

Once at the door, I tuck myself in behind him, slipping

my hand into his pocket and getting his key. I let my hand rummage into his pocket deeply, stroking along his length and fondling his balls. He sighs and lifts his arms, leaning in against the door, supporting himself as I play with him through his pocket. He bites his bottom lip to stifle a moan, and I pull my hand from his trousers and wave the key at him, putting it in the lock and opening the door.

Secure on the other side, I again launch myself against him, pushing him against the wall, his hands back over his head, and my lips back on his. I push my feet between his and manoeuvre his legs apart. I take the tie around his neck in my hand and tug on it; it loosens in my grasp. I break the kiss to look at the knot on the tie as I untie it, tugging it from around his neck. He looks at me through eyes hooded with desire and holds his hands out in front of him. I slip the tie around his outstretched wrists and bind them together tightly. He puts them back above his head and leans in for another kiss.

I respond to him greedily, my lips crushing against his, my tongue lapping over his as they dance together in our mouths. I want this man, and what's more, I want him naked. Hell, I want us both naked, the temptation to have my bare nipples pressed against his broad chest is just too much to resist. I pull his shirt free from his pants and start to undo the buttons. I move my lips from his, nibbling along his jaw until I reach his neck. A moan slips from his lips as my mouth makes contact with the tender skin just below his ear. I stop, lifting my head to look at him. I stare at him, keeping direct eye contact while I undo the rest of his buttons and flick the sides of his shirt apart, exposing his chest roughly. I run my hand across his jaw, over his lips, and down his masculine chest with a smattering of dark, dirty fair hair, right down to the little happy trail that leads into the front of his pants with the promise of something enticing. He sucks in a breath and holds it as my fingers go lower.

We both look down as I skim my palm over his swollen crotch, his held breath coming out in a throaty moan. I crush my lips against his again. My hands reach for his bound wrists, still above his head as I press my still-covered breasts against him, the friction of contact and fabric making my nipples stiffen to hard little pebbles. My hands move to his bare sides, grabbing at his skin, needing him closer as his own hands drop. He loops his restrained arms around my back, pulling me tighter against him.

Encased in his bound arms and flat against his chest, I can't resist when he nibbles my bottom lip and then nuzzles against the skin on my neck. I groan at the sensations washing over me, wanting more of him. I need to take back control and I break contact from him, dipping and ducking out from underneath his looped arms.

"Ah, ah, ah!" I scold, reaching for the hem of my top. "Do you want to see more?" I ask him, pausing with my top gathered, ready to pull off.

"You know I do," he replies huskily.

"Arms!" I warn, and he leans back against the wall and puts his arms back over his head, waiting. I lick my lips and slowly pull the top off over my head, dropping it to the floor. His inky black eyes sparkle with lust, and I reach behind me to unhook my bra. When I let it slip from my shoulders and down my arms, he hums in appreciation at seeing my ample breasts spill free. His breathing speeds up, and I slowly move in, brushing against him again, my nipples gently tickled by his chest hair. I skim myself against him, bare chest to bare breasts, and my lips lock with his once more, my hands again at his sides, pulling him towards me. I need to feel him closer.

As his tongue tangles with mine, again, his arms come down around me, and he pulls me tight against him. His lips trace across mine and to my neck and bare shoulder. He nibbles my skin, sucking it harshly into his mouth. He's marking me. I dig my nails into his back, and he bites down harder with a low moan, keeping me pressed against him.

"Mmmm... That's not how this is meant to work!" I warn him on an aroused sigh.

He lifts his head and looks at me with a smirk. "You can punish me for it later!"

I reach up for his head and grab a fistful of hair. "Oh, I will. You can bet on it!"

"I'm counting on it!"

I pull his head back, tuck my hands under his arms, and shove them back over his head away from me. I take a step back, letting my eyes roam over him. He shoots me a predatory look and lets his eyes feast on me in return.

I grin and walk away from him towards the bed. He looks at me when I pause and turn back to him.

"Crawl," I command.

He holds out his bound wrists as though they explain everything. I shrug and look at him again. "Crawl."

He keeps his back against the wall, kicks off his shoes, and sinks to his knees. His eyes never leave mine as he does. He finally comes to rest at my feet and again holds his hands out to me expectantly.

I take a step back from him and look at him intently. "I'm not sure you can be trusted to behave without your hands bound!"

He raises his eyebrows suggestively, and my pussy clenches. Shit, this guy is trouble: submissive with a hot streak of defiant alpha. A positively explosive combination. I hold his look before stepping toward him and reaching for his bound wrists. I untie him, slipping the tie around the back of my neck, keeping it to hand, just in case.

"Shirt off," I instruct, and his shirt slips off his body, gracing me with an unobstructed view. He is glorious. A broad chest and shoulders, toned without being obviously muscular, and a dappling of body hair a fraction darker than that on his head. He rubs a hand across his chest absently and looks up at me through thick lashes. The intensity of his gaze takes my breath away, and for a split second; I forget just how much I want control.

"And the rest," I tell him.

He grins. "And you," he insists.

"Together," I state in compromise and reach for the waist of my skirt, unzipping it. He reaches for his fly. Undoing the buttons on his jeans, he pulls them down his hips, over his legs to the floor before kicking them to the side. I let my skirt drop and pool at my feet.

We both stand there in our underwear, him in his tented cotton boxers and me in my lacy thong and stockings. He licks his lips as his eyes roam over my lower half before he takes a step towards me. He pauses before me, silently waiting for permission to do what he wants to. I gaze up at him and close the last of the space between us. I crush my lips against his. His hands find my ass and pull me tight against him, his hard cock pressing against my stomach.

As his tongue duels with mine, I wrap my arms around his neck. His hands grip my ass firmly and I'm hoisted up. Instinctively, my legs go around his hips as I cling on. His cock is now pressed hard against my throbbing pussy.

"This isn't how it's meant to go!" I breathe against his lips.

"So, stop me," he challenges and presses his lips to mine again. A fight begins inside me. The lust and the need I have for him versus the need to dominate and control. I'm really not sure which one I want to win more. I pull myself tighter against him and lose myself in the feeling of his lips on mine, his length against my sex, and how delicious this is.

His hands slide from my ass and up my back as he keeps a firm hold on me. With his arms encircling me, he backs up to the bed and collapses backwards, taking us both to the mattress. I pry myself off his chest and sit up on his hips, his cock still resting firmly against my wet sex.

"Do you trust me?" I grin at him.

His hands run over my stocking-covered thighs and come to rest on my hips, grabbing me as he grinds up against me. "Maybe." He smirks, quirking an eyebrow at me.

I slip the tie from around my neck again. "Wrists," I say as I hold the tie out in front of me, expecting him to put his arms out to me. He does. He smiles, and I wrap the tie around them, tying it tightly. I place them back on his stomach and lean over him, trapping them between us.

I kiss him hard and hungrily, letting him know exactly how I'm feeling. The lust I have bubbling over makes me feverish. I kiss across his jaw and down his neck. I nibble on his earlobe and delight in the growl that rumbles through him. It spurs me on, and I can't help but dig my teeth into his shoulder. He groans. "It's a good job you bound my hands, or I wouldn't be able to control myself right now," he warns. His appreciation of my actions only makes me bolder; I suck and nip at his flesh, marking him, claiming him as mine. He bites his lip and moans.

I release my mouth's hold on his shoulder and push myself up on his chest, grabbing his wrists before leaning back over him as I push them back over his head.

"You'd better behave," I warn him as I start to kiss my way down the side of his abdomen. He squirms beneath me. "Stay still!" I shoot him a glare.

He grins back at me. "It tickles!" He smiles and grinds his hips against me. I sink my teeth into his side, and a hiss erupts from him. I gaze in his direction and watch him watching me intently. I lift my head and warn again, "I told you to stay still."

"You're making it hard," he replies.

I grind against his hips, pressing myself tightly against his throbbing cock. "I know." I grin back at him and return to my kisses and nibbles along his side before moving to his mouth. I start with a lick across his lips, kissing down over his chin and neck, and then start to nip and suck across his chest muscles. Finally, my mouth reaches his right nipple, and I surround it, sucking it into my mouth. A rumbling growl resonates from him. He arches his back and meets my glance as I look up at him, his gaze heady with lust and full of desire. Warmth pools between my legs, and my lacy underwear is soaked. His stare is amplified, and I know he can feel the reaction he's creating in me too. "Don't you dare," I warn.

"You're testing my limits!"

"That's the idea." I smirk at him and move to his left nipple. He groans, and his hands move so his arms cover his face as he attempts to keep control of himself. I want to push him. I want him to make a move. I want to know just how much it will take. I want him to challenge me. I graze his nipple with my teeth, and I know what's coming a fraction of a second before it happens.

He lifts himself off the bed to sit up, taking me with him. His bound hands do nothing to stop him circling his arms around me. His mouth possesses me, and he pulls me tight against him. I melt in against him, my body naturally responding to his whether I want it to or not. Not that there's any doubt that I want it to. He grinds himself against me, and soon, my senses are swimming. Everything is lost other than my need for him.

"Untie me," he pants against my lips when he breaks our kiss. He unhooks his arms from around me and puts his hands in front of me expectantly. Normally, I would hesitate, but there is just something about him that prevents me from doing so. My fingers fumble against the knots in the tie as I try to get it off hastily. The instant his wrists are unbound, he runs his fingers through my long loose curls and pulls my face back to his as his lips possess mine once more.

I circle my arms around his waist, my nails digging into the skin on his lower back. His lips move across my face to my jaw before dipping to my neck. He instinctively finds that sweet spot below my ear, and my head falls back as I let out a moan. One hand runs down my back and sweeps around my waist before finding its home on my left breast.

His lips reach my shoulder, his hand kneading my breast. When he catches my nipple with his finger and thumb, his mouth's force on my shoulder increases. He's marking me like I marked him. Part of me wants to stop him, but the other part wants to surrender to the sensations he can generate in me, new and unbridled. I dig my nails hard into his flesh, not realising just how deeply until a hiss sounds from him, and his mouth releases my shoulder. "You're determined to leave marks, aren't you, kitten?" His nickname rings in my ears, and I lift my head to stare at him. "What's wrong?" he asks.

"Nothing, it's... silly."

He lifts his hand to my chin and kisses the tip of my nose. "It's not silly. Tell me."

I find his gaze comforting, and I want to explain. "You called me kitten, and my name is Kat. I'm Katriona," I tell him.

"You're such a little sex kitten. I just knew it would fit you." He smiles. "And for the record, I'm Mike. I'd like to hear my name on your lips when I make you come, my little Kat," he whispers before owning my mouth with his once more.

Suddenly, the space between us is too great. Our only barrier is our underwear, but it's too much and I can't take it. I push him back. I need to feel his skin against mine completely. I need to feel him—on me, in me. Placing a trail of kisses along his abdomen, I slowly make my way downward, tracing the line of hair from his belly button that disappears below the waistband of his underwear. I gaze up at him and pause, my fingers lightly resting at his hips, waiting for him to stop me.

"Do it," he replies to my unspoken question. I don't falter in pulling his boxers down over his hips and thighs; he lifts his ass from the bed to help me. He raises his feet and kicks them to the side. My eyes roam over the sight of him lying naked on the bed in front of me. His cock bobs against his stomach, as though he can feel my gaze like a soft caress. I'm hypnotised by it, unable to resist it. I have to taste him and dip my head towards him and run my tongue along his length. His warm, soft skin is a delight on my tongue, and I long to savour more of him. I lift him in my hand and cover the head of his cock with my mouth, sucking him between my lips and relishing in his aroused sighs. I bathe his dick in licks, exploring all over his head, lapping the pre-cum leaking from the tip.

I bob my head up and down in a slow, sensual, teasing pace, each time allowing a little more of him to push into my throat.

"Oh, Jesus, Kat!" he exclaims, grabbing my shoulders roughly. I gaze up at him, and his cock slides from my wet mouth.

Suddenly, I'm pinned to the bed on my back and my lacy knickers are gone, torn from my body in one swift move. He leans over me, pushing his knee between my legs. I stare into his eyes as my legs naturally part for him. He presses himself against me, resting on his elbows so we have skin-to-skin contact from our chest to our pelvis, to our tangle of legs.

"You're going to scream for me, little Kat," he says, brushing my hair from my face and nuzzling against my neck. "And when you do, you're going to scream my name," he breathes against my ear.

A shiver travels up and down my spine, and the tip of Mike's cock nudges between my slick folds. With a small move of his hips, he finds my entrance and slowly slides himself home.

I can't help myself. I wrap myself around him. I hook my legs around the back of his thighs, and my hands stroke up his sides and hold on to his broad shoulders and back. He rocks his pelvis against mine. I feel every last inch of him buried inside me, moving deeper, filling me until I'm sure I'm about to burst with ecstasy.

He bruises my lips with his own and captures my moans as if he needs them to breathe, kissing each one from me. He's slowly increasing his pace, the extra movement causing a tickle between my nipples and his chest hair. He's managing to rub across my clit with every stroke, and I find a furious storm brewing between my legs. His breathing is picking up. He's right there with me, feeling that need, that lust, chasing that finishing line.

Like a rising crescendo in a symphony, his hips thrust into me more and more. Finally, I just can't contain it any longer. Stars start at the edges of my vision until I'm swallowed by a blinding light as wave after wave of orgasm crashes over me.

"Fuck, Mike!" I scream out as he thrusts hard into me. I want to come down from the experience, but he doesn't stop.

"That's it, Kat," he pants against my lips. "One more," he encourages, and the split second I'm coming down is replaced by another cataclysmic climax.

I pull him tight against me as he stiffens. A roar erupts from him as he is captured by his own orgasm. He leans back against me and kisses me tenderly as we both lie there, basking in the afterglow of what happened. My hands caress his back, and he strokes the side of my face.

After that night, I gave Mike my number. I always played safe men who were submissive, so the control was mine, but Mike is different. He's challenging, a little bit alpha male. As it turns out, he lives not far from me. We've seen each other a few times now. Who knows where things might lead?

Chapter Two

It's been a long time since I've had a man in my own home. I go to theirs, we have fun in hotels, but I've always tried to keep my sex life away from my personal space. So, having Mike here is a completely new experience for me. It's not the first time he's been in my house, but this is the first time he's been coming here exclusively for me to dominate him. There's something suddenly more intimate about the whole experience.

There's a knock at the door, and when I open it, he's standing there with a familiar cheeky grin on his face.

"Come in," I demand with a smirk, standing aside to let him in.

"Good evening, Mistress." He beams at me and plants a kiss on my cheek. I try not to smirk in the face of his impish charm. I know what he's doing, and I can't help but adore him for it. He's trying to lighten the mood and do as much as he can to make the experience easier on me.

"Strip," I command. He looks at me, and I know what he's thinking. "Yes, right here in the hallway."

Slowly, taking pleasure in teasing and flashing every last

inch of his skin, Mike starts to remove all of his clothing, just as he was told to, standing right there in my hall. When all of his glorious form is naked, he smiles and stands with his hands by his sides, daring me to look at all of him. I allow myself the indulgence, my eyes roaming over all of his form until my gaze finally reaches his impressive hard cock.

"On your knees," I demand.

He complies, never breaking his gaze from mine. He sinks down, his buttocks resting on his heels, looking up at me. I push my bare foot forward to him. "Kiss it," I tell him. He leans forwards and places his lips gently against the top of my foot. I glance down at him, and he catches the meaning in my raised eyebrow. He returns his attention to my foot and kisses it more tenderly, his tongue running along the side of my foot, and his lips nipping at my toes. I bite my bottom lip, enjoying the sensation already, desire moving from his lips on my feet directly to my pussy.

I pull that foot back and extend the other one for the same treatment. Mike wraps his lips around my toes and licks along my foot, and again, I feel every movement right through to my pussy. This man is already becoming my undoing. He's more than I had ever considered taking on previously. Both in the fact that he's not a typical submissive, and that I'm now out of my comfort zone having a man back in my house, getting under my skin, the same submissive to play with every time. The look he gives me as he rises on his knees and runs his hand up my inner leg and under my dress wipes away every hesitation. I grab his wrist and look at him with a hard stare.

"Excuse me? Were you invited to do anything other than kiss my feet?" I ask him.

He smirks at me, his eyes already full of lust. "No... *Miss*," he says, purposely pausing as if he had forgotten his place and needed to tack the last word on once he remembered.

"Is calling me your mistress causing you issues, little one?" I smile at him.

"It's not what I'd like to call you, Kitty Kat," he says defiantly. Something about how he rolls his tongue around my name makes me willing to forgive him and allow him this one concession.

"Fine," I concede. "As long as you show me respect as your dominant, I don't care what term you use to address me. But let's not overuse the 'Kitty Kat,' please."

He nods and sinks back until his butt rests on his heels again. "What would you like to do with me?" He smiles, holding his arms out to show himself off, his confidence coming off him in waves.

"Get upstairs." He goes to rise from his knees. "Ah! Ah! I didn't say you could get up now, did I?" The *'are you kidding me'* look he gives me is more reward than I had hoped for. He turns around on his hands and knees and crawls up the stairs as I commanded, with me following. I drink in the sight of his arse waving before me, and I know I'm going to enjoy making it a delicious shade of red.

He creeps up the stairs, and without asking, heads straight for my bedroom, with me admiring the view as he does. When he reaches beside the bed, he rests back on his heels and waits for me to say something more. I move to the large chest of drawers in the room, pull open the bottom drawer, and lift out my leather wrist and ankle restraints.

"On the bed. Face down," I instruct.

He rises, his hard cock standing proud in front of him, and he places himself onto the bed, face down, his head supported with his hand, his arm up on his elbow. He watches me as I move towards him with the restraints. I take the time to rub my fingers over his skin and place a chaste kiss against his inner wrists and ankles, buckling the cuffs tight.

He looks at me over his shoulder, silently asking what I'm going to do next. I move to the bottom of the bed and reach under the mattress, pulling out a sneaky little under-bed restraint system I have. I open the clip on his ankle cuff, connect it to the ring, and pull the strap tight, pulling Mike's ankle almost to the corner of the bed. I repeat the process on his other ankle, and then his two wrists. By the time I'm finished, he's a starfish, restrained tightly to the bed, face down. I stand beside him and let him watch as I strip out of my dress, bra, and knickers, letting them all fall to the floor as I delight in his lustful gaze.

"See anything you like?" I tease him.

"You know I do, kitten," he says on a sigh.

I grin at his admission of desire and walk towards the bed, climbing onto it, straddling him, and putting my backside down on top of his, my pussy perfectly in line with the crack of his arse. I grind myself against him, letting him feel that I'm already wet at the thought of having him here on my bed, naked. He groans when he feels my slickness against him. I lean over to him, my mouth by his ear, my breasts and stiff nipples pressed against his back. "Do you like that feeling?" I ask.

He moans. "Fucking right I do."

Now I begin the big tease.

I move against his back, making sure to trail the tips of my nipples against him. I start at his neck and plant a trail of soft kisses down under his ear, over his shoulder, and down his back. I kiss down along his side, knowing he's ticklish there, letting the heat of my breath blow across his skin. His ass muscles tighten, and he flexes against the bed. I lift my hand and give him a hard strike against his buttocks.

"Don't you dare dry hump my sheets, slut," I warn.

A soft growl ripples through Mike and causes goosebumps to rise on my skin. I have a need to find out just how much of a red arse he can handle now I see his reaction to my hand with a little name-calling. I move against him, changing my position, slipping down his back and coming to rest between his outspread legs. I can't resist giving his backside an extra slap as I do.

I lean forward, and I sink my teeth into his right buttock. I want to mark him, to brand him. I want to push him and see what he can take. I apply a gentle sucking pressure along with my teeth, knowing that a reddish-purple mark will rise on his skin. He moans, and again, his ass muscles tighten. I smack his left buttock.

I need to tease him, to tempt him, to prove submission is just what he needs. I run my hands along his inner thighs and crack them down hard on his ass cheeks. I repeat the action several times, caressing his thighs, soothing his skin, and increasing his need, fuelling my desires just as much as his.

After a few cycles of the tease, followed by the slaps, his ass is turning a nice shade of pink and starting to feel warm to the touch, but I know I can do better. I run my hands up his thighs again, and this time, instead of slapping his buttocks, I grab them firmly and spread them. His arsehole is exposed to me, and I lean forward and circle it with the tip of my tongue. Mike's initial jolt at the sensation quickly subsides to a low moan. His hips lift, and I feel him trying to move against my mouth.

I bury my face between his buttocks and lavish his arse with attention from my tongue. I can feel him moving against the bed. I know he's attempting to get the right kind of friction he needs to be able to jack himself off with my tongue fucking his arsehole, and it's the best reaction I could have hoped for. I stop and get off the bed. Mike groans and lifts his head to see what's going on.

"Kat?" he questions.

I grin. "Don't worry, I'm not done with you yet." I open a drawer and lift out three items: a butt plug, some lube, and a paddle. I move back to the bed, and I return to my position between Mike's legs.

"If you need me to stop, I will, okay?" I remind him.

"Do it, Kat!" he growls, lust filling his voice.

I rub my hand over his pink buttocks, open the lid on the lube, and dribble it between his ass cheeks. I rub my fingers down to his arsehole, pushing the lube against him, coating him.

I start to tease him, my lubed finger pushing into him, demanding entrance. The sound Mike makes when my index finger breaches that ring of muscle is beyond divine. It's a low, almost primal groan that makes my clit throb.

I spend a few moments fucking him with my finger, watching it with fascination as it disappears into him. After his hips attempt to fall into a rhythm with my finger, I smack him hard on the ass with my other hand.

"Stay still," I warn.

I rub the butt plug with some lube, with my spanking hand, and slip my finger from Mike's arse before replacing it with the butt plug. I'm done teasing, and I push it into his ass in one slow, firm movement. His previous guttural groan returns with new intensity, and the wetness of my pussy makes my thighs slick.

With the plug securely in place, I straddle Mike's restrained right leg and make sure he is very much aware of just how wet I am by rubbing my cunt on his leg, grinding it against him.

"Jesus, Kat..." he begins, but I don't let him finish the thought before I crack the paddle down hard on both buttocks. Mike hisses in pain, yet the flex of his hips afterwards suggests he's more turned on than I had hoped.

"You're a dirty little slut, aren't you?" I ask rhetorically. "I know how hard you are from having your ass filled, and now I'm going to punish you for it!" I inform him, shifting on his leg, reminding him of my wet pussy.

I begin paddling his ass further with earnest. I count each strike out loud, making sure almost every last one connects with the base of the butt plug, increasing the mixture of sensations Mike is experiencing.

By the time I've finished with the thirty lashes of the paddle, his arse looks like it's on fire it's so red, and Mike is writhing about on the bed seeking some kind of release. I move off the bed, putting the paddle away. I return to Mike's ankles and unclip them from the straps. I then do the same to his wrist cuffs. When I go to step back from the bed, Mike lunges, grabbing me and pulling me down on the bed beside him.

He puts me on my back and moves between my legs, using his body to cover mine, sinking his rock-hard dick into my cunt and his lips over mine to capture my groans of pleasure.

I fall asleep that night thoroughly sated, having been taken to the dizzying heights of orgasmic bliss several times by a hot alpha yet submissive male with a plugged arse.

Suddenly, this man in my house doesn't seem like such a bad idea after all.

Chapter Three

It's funny, I wouldn't have thought I could share my life and my friends with someone else after what I went through in my divorce. However, as time goes on, Mike just keeps worming his way more and more into my life, and what's more, I seem to be more and more comfortable letting him.

It's a nice weekend in March, and I'm in Liverpool having fun with some friends of mine at an annual event we all attend together. These are my good friends. The ones who know the most about me. The ones who are fully aware of how I met Mike, of how I spent my free time. They know I'm the 'kinky one' of the group, and they enjoy teasing me about how things are changing now that Mike is on the scene. I'll get my revenge. He laps up the fact that they wind me up about it, but I can always turn those tables.

We're sitting at the bar when Eipha asks us all if we want to go out for a meal to this great little Mexican place she's found. Jennifer, Maggie, and Annabella agree, but I explain that I need to wait for Mike, and I have no idea when he'll show up.

"Bring him!" Eipha insists, and the rest of the gang looks at me expectantly.

I smirk back at her. "Eipha, I have one word for you... Pegging..."

Her face lights up with glee. "Fuck, yes!" She's practically rubbing her hands in delight, keen for more details. "Details. I need details!"

I laugh. "You know the way I've been seeing him for a while now? Well he's a filthy one, he likes bum love and being in my knickers. As in wearing my knickers."

Maggie snorts and goes red. "Jesus, Kat. Too much information!"

Jennifer just grins and knocks back her drink.

"This is just making my life right now you, know this?" Eipha laughs.

I shake my head with a grin. "I'm so glad this is working out so well for you!" Just as I'm laughing at the girls' reaction, my phone chirps with a text.

You should come outside.

I chew my lip as I read it.

"Ohh, must be the bum lover! Do we get to meet him?" Eipha asks.

"Go have your meal. I'll meet you in the hotel bar later, if I'm not too busy." I smile as I get up from my seat and head for the main door of the lobby.

I walk out into the cool March evening air and look around the car park. I can't see him, and then I see a figure getting out of what I recognise to be Mike's car. I cross the car park calmly and throw my arms around him when I finally reach him.

"Hello, stranger." I smile at him as he nuzzles into my neck.

"I've missed you," he murmurs against my shoulder.

I stand there for a while, relishing the arms that I have missed for a few days before releasing him and stepping back. I place my hand in his and head back to the hotel's main doors, with him beside me.

We walk into the lift in silence, just casting meaningful looks in each other's direction every few minutes. Just as the lift is arriving on my floor, I look at him.

"The girls asked if we would be back down later. I told them I didn't know, since I would be deep in your ass while you wear my knickers." I smirk and depart the lift, waiting for him to collect himself and follow me.

In a second, he's beside me.

"You don't mind if they know what a little whore you are, do you?" I ask, feigning innocence.

"It's all good." He smiles back. I really have met my match with Mike; the further I push, the more he stands his ground, relishing each challenge to his alpha tendencies.

The door to the room closes and Mike drops down on the bed on his back. I move to the other side of the bed and flop down beside him on my stomach. His hand is instantly on my back, rubbing me soothingly. He knows that just his hands on me is enough to turn me on, even with a gesture as chaste as this one.

"Mmmm, that feels nice," I say, soothed by his touch. His large hands continue to stroke my back. But it isn't enough. I need more, and knowing Mike, he knows exactly what he's doing. I push myself off the bed and watch his face as I slip off my bra, without removing anything else, and throw it in his direction. I grab the tops of my leggings and knickers from underneath my dress and yank them down. I step out of them, leaving them in a pile on the floor, joining Mike back on the bed, face down as I had been before.

Mike's hand returns to my back. His touch is firmer. His hand skims lower on my back, and I know I've affected him as much as he's affecting me. His hand creeps lower, and my dress rides up, exposing my bare backside. He cups my buttocks firmly. I groan and push my ass back against his hand. He grabs my flesh harshly and rolls onto his side, tucking himself in against my side. His hand dips between my legs, and I part them to allow him the access he's seeking.

Instantly, his fingers find my wet cunt and slide between my labia, settling on my clit. His lips touch my bare shoulder, and a low growl ripples over my skin when he finds me already so slick for him.

I lift my head and move towards him. I need to capture his mouth with my own. As soon as my lips touch his, Mike slips a finger inside me. I moan against his mouth as he licks along my lips and penetrates them with his tongue. All day my thoughts have been consumed with anticipation of the night ahead and a desperate desire to feel Mike's touch. It doesn't take long for him to make me lose control. As soon as he slides a second finger inside me, I can't help but clench around him.

When he feels my orgasm subside, he removes his fingers from my pussy and lifts them to his lips, licking them clean of my juices.

"Damn, you taste good!" He smiles, taking exaggerated licks from his fingers. I move on the bed, forcing him to lie on his back again. I indulge myself with a kiss, tasting myself on his lips, then I move again. Before he realises what I'm doing, I turn to face his feet and straddle his head, quickly lowering my pussy towards his face. "Since I taste so good, perhaps you should get a better opportunity to savour me," I tease, just as my cunt makes contact with his nose and mouth.

A muffled groan comes from below me, and his hands suddenly grip my thighs, pulling me against him harshly. His tongue works its way along my pussy, teasing, pushing inside me before returning to my clit. His nose is pressed against my ass, nuzzling against it when he plunges his tongue inside me and pressing into my pussy when he laps at my clit.

It's not long and I'm coming again. My juices coat Mike's face. He knows how wet he gets me and loves feeling it against him. I lean forward and undo the button on his jeans and reach inside to free his rock-hard cock. When my fingers make contact with his skin, another groan vibrates through my sensitive cunt. I press my body against Mike's and take his cock into my greedy mouth.

His right hand disappears from my thigh, and I feel it working my wetness towards my asshole. I moan around Mike's cock, and it pulses in my mouth. I'm here sitting on his face, and still my alpha needs to take some control. His finger now pushes against my ass, seeking entry as his mouth latches around my clit for him to suck on it.

He overloads my senses when his finger slips into my ass and he starts to fuck it. I come again, crying out around his cock as he keeps me impaled on him at both ends of me. I let him fall from my mouth with a pop and grab him tightly in my fist. I give him a hard squeeze.

"Remember who is in control here, slut!" I pant as he continues to work my clit and ass. I dig my nails into his balls roughly and another, louder moan erupts beneath me.

"Oh, you liked that, huh?" I taunt him. He bites on my clit, just enough for me to feel a sharp sting. I moan and grind against him roughly, while slapping his hard cock, reminding him he needs to let it go and give in to me. He rubs the hand he kept on my thigh over me soothingly. I know he is granting me the control I crave. I grind against him and let him lick and finger fuck me to one more orgasm before I finally get off him.

I grab my discarded knickers from the floor, returning to the bed to use them to wipe my juices from his soaked face. I kiss him hard, a silent thank you for the multiple orgasms he's given me so far, and to thank him for his submission.

"Strip," I order when I pry my lips from his. Silently and without complaint, Mike rises from the bed and makes a show of stripping off every last item of clothing. I sit and wait, enjoying the sight of more and more of his amazing skin on display.

When his last item of clothing is discarded, he stands in front of me defiantly, his cock bobbing proudly in front of him. I hold out my hand, dangling my knickers in his direction. "Get these on." I smile.

He glances at the knickers I've been wearing all day and just used to wipe his face. He licks his lips and takes them from me, stepping into them, locking his gaze with mine as he pulls the red lacy panties up his legs, over his thighs, and into place covering his cock, balls, and ass.

I bite my lips, delighting in the sight of Mike's cock straining against my knickers.

"God, I love it when you're a little slut for me," I breathe out. His dick bobs when he hears the word 'slut.' I love the effect it has on him when I call him names like that. There's a real thrill in seeing his head bow slightly and his eyes glaze over in desire. It's the small, seemingly insignificant elements of submission I love the most.

I stand and move towards him, feeling like a big cat after its prey. I give him a wicked grin and lead him to the small table in the room. I line him up near it and push him by the shoulder, indicating that I want him to bend forward over the table.

He complies, leaning forward, his stomach resting against the tabletop, his rear end sticking out behind him. I grab my long silky scarf from the back of the chair and fasten it around one wrist, loop it around the single support in the middle of the table, and fasten it finally to his other wrist. He's now stuck there, bent over the table. My victim, ready to take whatever I desire.

I reach between his legs and rub his cock through the red lace that confines it. A low rumble escapes from Mike at my touch. I smack his backside hard, and then move away from him to where my bag is at the bottom of the wardrobe. I lift out two things: my strap-on, in its harness, and the pair of knickers I wore all day yesterday. I remove my dress, hang it up, enjoying that I can take my time and let him wait, anticipation building within him.

I slip into the strap-on harness, drawing it slowly up my legs as Mike watches from the table. I take my time in securing it in place and adjusting the straps. I then step in front of him, hold my realistic-looking faux cock near his face and demand, "Suck it, whore."

His lips part, and I push the tip of my dick into his mouth. My hand goes to the back of his head as I push the strap-on further towards his throat. When he's like this, I own him, and I don't hesitate to make sure he completely understands that.

I give him a moment to acclimate to me in his mouth

before I start to thrust, my cock pushing a little further in with every stroke.

"Look how pretty you look with my knickers on and my dick in your mouth. Being my filthy little whore suits you so well!" I tease him, and he moans around my dick. I love to take him like this. I love to see him accepting me and feel him resisting me less and less with each penetration of his slutty little mouth.

I give him one final rough thrust, and he gags before I pull out of his mouth. I place my worn knickers under his nose and let him smell them. I want him to know that they have been worn; I know he gets off on it. I'm not sure he's aware that I know, but he soon will be.

"Do you smell that, slut?" I ask.

He looks up at me. "Yes, Miss," he replies.

"You like that, don't you?" I smile.

A slight blush flushes his cheeks and he licks his lips. If I was looking, I know his rock-hard cock would have twitched in appreciation.

"I know you like how my knickers smell after I've worn them, you filthy little deviant. Now, open wide," I command, shoving the balled-up panties at his lips. When he opens his mouth for me, I cram them in, gagging him on them. His eyes are hooded with lust. I can't resist the look on his face. I know he wants more, and to deny him would be cruel.

I walk behind him, grab the lube from the dressing table behind him as I go, pop the lid, and start to make sure my dick is nice and wet for Mike's ass. Normally, I would tease him a little, applying lube to his asshole with my fingers, but this time, I feel the need to be a little bit cruel. I apply a liberal drop to my cock head instead and begin to rub it against his arse, giving a firm push, relentlessly begging entrance.

Tonight, I don't want to tease him. Tonight, I want to be merciless. I don't thrust and tempt him, looking for entry. I demand it. I keep the tip of my cock pressed against his asshole and I push. I keep pressing until, with a loud muffled groan from Mike, my cock slides inside, right up to the fake balls that hang below my fake cock. I don't waste any time, I don't let him adjust; I need to take him hard and rough. I need to possess him. I pull back until the tip of my cock is almost out of his ass before I slide back in to the hilt. More muffled moans sound from Mike. I repeat the tease of almost withdrawing and sinking back in over and over.

The more I hear him enjoying it, the more I feel him raising his arse to meet me, the more it spurs me on, and the more I repeatedly pound deep and hard into him, fucking him like my life depends on it as a frenzy of lust takes over me. A sheen of sweat covers both of us as I keep riding him hard. I always position my strap-on in such a way that it sits almost where a real cock would hang against my body. In doing so, pounding into someone like this always creates a delicious friction through me to my clit. The wave of pleasure starts, my nails dig into his hips, and my thrusts become faster and more erratic, urgent. Soon, I'm crying out as I drive deep into Mike one last time, my own orgasm ripping through me, slickness coating the tops of my thighs because of it.

I remain there for a few minutes, deep in Mike's arse, my knees just about holding me up. I'm distracted when my phone chirps with a message. I slowly ease out of him and step towards my phone. The girls have made it back to the bar and want to know if I'm too busy to come down. I feel like having a little fun with this, so I text back that I'll be down shortly. I grab a butt plug from my bag, add a little lube, and move back to Mike, sliding the plug into his well fucked asshole with relative ease. I move to his head and pull the knickers from his mouth, bending to kiss him hard on the lips. I move back behind him and stoop to his feet.

"Lift your leg," I command, tapping his right ankle. I slip my knickers over Mike's foot and repeat the demand on his left ankle. I stand and slide my knickers up his legs, pulling them into place over his cock and filled arse. I give him a hard smack on the buttocks and untie his hands.

"Come on, get dressed. The girls are back, and we're going to the bar for a drink or two with them."

He straightens. "Like this?" he asks, his hands rubbing over his still rock-hard cock. I look at him and rethink my plan of action just a little. With my own cock still bobbing between my legs, I kneel before him, thighs parted, and dip the front of my knickers to free his cock. I wrap my lips around him and suck him deep into my mouth. He groans, his eyes close, and his head tilts back. His hand grabs the base of his cock firmly, and I let him slip from my mouth again. He begins to fist his hard dick furiously in front of me, and within minutes, he comes hard, shooting his load over my tits. I keep my eyes on his and rub his essence into my skin, over my breasts and stomach, especially my knickers.

"I'll spend the evening knowing that you are wearing my knickers with a fat plug in your arse, and you can spend it knowing that I'm wearing you all over me," I tell him and rise to get dressed. Mike grabs me at the waist as I go past and pulls me against him hard, kissing me forcefully.

"And fucking sexy you look wearing it too," he tells me as he nuzzles into my neck. I nudge him away from me.

"Get ready," I demand and smirk as I watch him tuck

his already-hardening cock back into my knickers and walk towards where his clothes were discarded on the floor..

I doubt we'll stay long in the bar. Both of us are too wound up and ready to have our hands all over each other, but it will make for a very interesting hour or so of foreplay while we do.

Chapter Four

I have been planning this particular adventure for a month now. I need to head to Birmingham on some business, and Mike suggested it would be the perfect opportunity for us to have a little fun.

I'm in my hotel room, waiting for him to arrive. I'm wearing strappy heels, stockings, a silk shift dress, and nothing else. There's a knock at the door, and I open it. When he walks into the room, I can't help but smile. He doesn't know what I have planned for him, but I know he's going to love it.

I walk over to him and kiss him, wrapping my arms around him. I hate admitting it, but it's getting to the point where I miss him when he's not around. But I also know the reason for this visit, and I'm not going to deprive him or myself of it for much longer. I push him back and look at the lust written all over his face.

"Strip," I demand of him.

He smirks at me and pulls his t-shirt over his head slowly, letting me savour his exposed skin more and more as he knows I like to do. He's always told me how much he gets off on admiring my naked form, but I don't think he truly understands just how much I get a kick out of exactly the same thing.

I lick my lips, captivated by the broad chest and shoulders that have been exposed for my visual delights. Mike pauses and looks at me, discarding his t-shirt on the floor beside him. I smirk and shake my head.

"And the rest," I demand. My eyes follow his hands to the top of his jeans, and I wait. I already know he's hard for me. I know he has been before he even walked into the room, but it's the pleasure I get out of this particular tease. Me standing here fully clothed, while he stands naked in front of me, his cock hard. There is a real pleasure for me in knowing I'm the one who got him like that.

He pops the button, undoes the zip, and looks straight at me, almost daring me to say something about what he's going to flash. I look at him and raise an eyebrow, and that's all it takes for him to drop his jeans and boxers to the floor, stepping out of them and his shoes and kicking them all aside.

His hands cover his cock, and he looks at me again. "Is this what you wanted?" he asks.

I cast a glance down at the socks still on his feet. "Everything, slut. Every last item of clothing. And I don't remember saying you could cover yourself with your hands."

His eyes go down to his hands, and then to the floor and his feet. His hands lower, his cock freely pointing upwards when he moves to remove his socks. When he stands straight again, he leaves his hands by his sides. My pussy clenches to see him there, ready for me, and so clearly willing to do whatever I want.

I swallow and take a deep breath. "Get on your hands and knees," I command.

Mike sinks to his knees before me and puts his hands on the floor in front of him. I take the chance to admire his ass in this position; one I fully intend to make good use of later, but until then, I'm going to have a little more fun. I put a foot out in front of him and I tell him to lick it. He glances up at me with heavy-lidded, lust-filled eyes, leaning forward and placing his lips around my big toe as best he can around my shoe, and sucks.

I'm not sure if it's that I have a particular fetish for feet, but there is something intoxicatingly powerful about the sight of a man naked on his hands and knees kissing and sucking on your feet. I watch him, almost hypnotised, every single touch of his on my foot seemingly sent directly to my pussy, making me wet, needy, and wanting so much more. I swap feet and let him lavish the other one with just as much attention as the first.

There's a very specific task I want to achieve with Mike today. He let it slip to me some time ago that he has never been able to come with oral sex. Sure, he's been able to push himself with a hand job, or other elements, to eventually come in a woman's mouth, but never from her mouth directly. Obviously, this is something I want to claim as mine. I want to be the first woman to drive him to climax with just her mouth, so that no matter what happens between us, any time in the future, all blow jobs will remind him of the woman who could. It's a little narcissistic, but I'm a dominant. Claiming firsts just has that appeal, and while I'm usually claiming some firsts in the games I've played in the past, there's a striking freshness to claiming a first of this kind.

I lift my foot from the floor in front of him and push him back.

"Ah-ah-ah!" I scold. "Let's not get carried away, my little slut."

He gives me that look, the one I get when I call him names like 'slut.' I know the effect it has on him and how much he enjoys it.

"Heel." I smirk as I strut past him and head for where my usual bag of tricks is. I grin when I see he's crawling on his hands and knees behind me.

He looks at me, waiting to see what I will pull from the bag. We've talked about a lot of different things he would be willing to try, but I have purposefully not mentioned anything about what I'm going to do this time around.

I lift Mike's favourite lingerie of mine out of the bag. I can see the cogs in his mind moving. He knows this situation well enough to know it couldn't possibly be as simple as me stripping off in front of him and putting it on for him. He understands there will be a catch, and I'm about to tell him what it is.

"Stand," I tell him. I pull a pair of stockings from the pile. I move towards him, circling them around his neck, letting them brush over his skin before using them to pull him closer to me as I kiss him hard and deep, making my lust for him abundantly clear.

"These are for you," I tell him when I pull back from our kiss. He looks at me, and I feel his cock bob between us. He's definitely going to enjoy this. I kneel before him, his cock just inches from my mouth. I wet my lips with my tongue in a move made purely to exaggerate the possibility of the situation. I part the stockings, setting one beside me, and start to carefully open one out between my fingers. I motion for him to lift his foot and step into the stocking, which he does without hesitation. I delight in running my hand over his leg, from ankle to thigh, as I pull the hold-up into position. I smooth it out around his thigh, letting my fingers gently caress the fold of his buttock at the back, my wrist just grazing against his balls as I do.

Mike groans, his eyes close, and his head drops back a fraction. I'm loving every second of blissful torture this seems to be forcing on him. I let my hands slide back down over his stocking-clad leg as I retrieve the other stocking from the floor beside me and begin the same process on his other leg, caressing him softly as I cover him in the sheer material and lace.

As I stand, I see the tip of his cock glisten with precum, and I can't resist taking it in my hand to give it a cleansing lick.

"Fuck," Mike moans. I smile and stand back, returning to the lingerie I had lifted out of the bag. Mike knows what's in store for him now. He watches as I pull the lacy panties from the small pile and unfold them. "You know why I like these?" I ask him.

He shakes his head.

"Because later, they are just neat enough for me to be able to ball them up and put them into your mouth while I fuck your greedy little ass. Can't have the hotel complaining about the noise." I smile and rub the knickers across his lips before I drop to my knees in front of him again and help him into the panties I have, pulling them up and having them straining under the weight of his throbbing cock.

The sight of him in my stockings and knickers has me practically spontaneously combusting. I'm not sure when the game changed, but it did. It used to be that this was all about me giving the pleasure, taking what I wanted and needed in the process. Now, doing all of these things with

Mike makes me just as wanton as he is. The ground is always shifting beneath my feet now, and I'm loving the excitement and the thrill of it all.

I return to the pile I have waiting for him, and I lift my half-cup basque, the one that matches the panties, and I tell him to turn around. I wrap my arms around his waist, taking the liberty of placing small kisses across his back between his shoulder blades as I do.

"Put your arms in," I tell him as I hold the basque out in front of him.

He slips his arms into the straps, and I wrap the garment around him and start to fasten it up the back. When the hooks are all in place, I fasten the attached suspenders to his stockings and then stand back to admire my handy work.

I'm not sure I can describe how it feels to see a man wearing my underwear. Maybe it's the stark contrast between this broad-shouldered, hairy-chested, otherwise alpha man, and the delicate lace and sheer material that surrounds him, or it's knowing that where his hard cock now sits was once pressed firmly against my wet pussy. There's just something about it that makes me feel empowered and incredibly turned on.

I can't help myself. I pounce, driving my lips hard against his, wrapping my arms around his neck. He wraps his arms tightly around my waist, pulling me in against him, pressing me against his hard lace-covered cock. I feel the need in his body. I can read his want and it matches my own, but I'm not ready to let him get what he wants quite so easily. My little game isn't over just yet.

I bend him over and tell him to get on his hands and knees on the bed. I watch as he does, drinking in every movement of his masculine form. I move behind him and slap my hand down hard on his backside. He hisses at the sting and presses back against my hand when I caress his buttock to soothe his burning skin. Before he can settle into the sensation too much, I crack my hand back down on his backside again and caress over the warmed skin once more.

I return to my bag of goodies once again and lift out a large butt plug with a remote control and some lube. I slip the remote into the top of my hold-ups and step back towards Mike's ass. Now I start the real teasing. I smack him hard on the ass again, this time slipping my hand between his legs to cup his balls, also running my hand over his hard shaft. He groans and shifts his hips to try and grind against my hand. Knowing he is so ready for me makes me wet. I know where this is leading, even if he doesn't yet. I need to taste him; it's practically a physical need within me now.

"Look at you grinding against my hand like a common little whore," I mock. "Tell me you're a whore, and I might just let you come."

"I'm a whore, Miss," he breathes.

"Sorry, I think I missed that. What are you?" I say, letting him rut against my hand a little more, rubbing him more firmly, giving him almost enough friction, but not quite.

"I'm your common little whore, Miss," he calls out.

I remove my hand and spank his ass again.

"Indeed you are my little whore, and do you know what happens to whores?" I ask him with an evil smirk.

I roughly pull aside his panties exposing his tight asshole. I pop the top on the lube and apply it to the valley between his buttocks, and using my fingers, liberally rub it around his entrance, teasing it every once in a while by slipping my fingertip in, making sure he is very well slicked up.

"Oh, God..." he moans.

I add a little more lube to my hand and coat the plug with it, then I introduce it to Mike's ass. "That's right, good little whores get taken hard anyway I want," I remind him as I push the plug into him in one slow move. I know what this is doing to him, but I know he'll get off on the relentless penetration. I intend to take him to the brink of desire before I even get my lips around his amazing cock.

I cover his arse again with the sheer material of the panties and give him one last hard smack for good measure, making sure to connect with the base of the plug as I do. The long moan he lets out tells me that I have achieved the level of wanton need in him that I had hoped to. Little does he know, I'm not even remotely done yet.

"Get on your back in the middle of the bed," I demand. Mike does exactly as he's told. He knows what he wants, and he knows I'm going to give him what he needs. "Hands on the headboard."

Once his hands are where they're meant to be, I take great pleasure in removing my dress and revealing to him that I have nothing on but my stockings beneath it. The look of lust and desire on his face is almost enough to make me just straddle him then and there, but I have a prize in mind still, and I intend to collect it.

I approach the bed at his feet and kiss them softly, putting my hands on either side of his legs and slowly creeping up over his stocking-covered skin with a peppering of indulgent kisses. Once I reach the top of his thighs, I cup my mouth over his balls, my hot breath radiating through the thin fabric covering them. Mike's hips rise against my mouth, and I feel his eyes burning into me.

I look up at him and meet his gaze as I pull the knickers down and free his now-engorged cock. I lick from his exposed balls to the head of his dick without breaking eye contact.

"Jesus!" he hisses, and without waiting any further, I sink my mouth over him and take him deep into my throat. His muscles tighten at the sensation. I begin to slowly work my way up and down his shaft, teasing it with my tongue, constantly looking at him, making sure he sees just how much I enjoy having him in my mouth. Just how much I want to taste more of him. Just as his body starts to match my movements with its own, I break my contact with his cock and move to his nipple, laying my naked flesh against his side and wrapping my leg over his.

My half-cup basque has his nipples fully exposed for me, and I waste no time in sucking the closest one into my mouth and lapping at it with my tongue. Mike hisses. I know he's enjoying it; I just need to take him that extra mile. As I suck and nibble on his chest, I reach for the remote control tucked in my stocking and turn it on. A small vibration starts in the plug in Mike's ass, and he groans, his body grinding against thin air.

I tease his other nipple between my finger and thumb, and when I know he's wound up just enough, I move back down his body and take his cock in my mouth again. This time, I'm met by thrusting. He needs release and I fully intend to give it to him. I press the button on the remote again, and the sensations increase within the plug. Again, Mike's hips start to move, meeting my mouth with every lick, pushing back into my throat further and further with each stroke. I lap at him hungrily. I need this now; this is pushing me towards my satisfaction as much as his.

Mike is panting. I know he's close, so I press the remote one last time and set it to the highest vibrations it can manage. I let my hands roam over his thighs and cup his balls again, then move my fingers to the base of the plug, grabbing it through the sheer fabric to start to move it slightly in and out of his ass, fucking him with it, increasing that delicious sensation that only comes from the feeling of having your arsehole fucked.

Suddenly, Mike's hands are in my hair. They push on the back of my head, holding me against him as he thrusts into my mouth in an irregular, spasming rhythm. He's moaning loudly, and suddenly he explodes in my mouth, crying out as he climaxes hard, filling my mouth with his cum, letting me taste every last drop of him. I swallow the first few spurts as they flow down the back of my throat, but I then pull back slightly, letting him finish on my tongue instead. I hold it in my mouth and let him finish, squeezing the last drops from him with my lips then letting his sated dick lie flat against his stomach. I move back up along his side and crush my lips against his.

His tongue enters my mouth, and I know he's tasting himself on my tongue too. He groans and pulls me hard against him, his tongue lapping at mine, savouring how he tastes in my mouth. I've claimed my prize, I press the off button on the plug to still it, and he keeps me drawn tight against him. His lips part from mine, and he licks the last of his taste from them.

"Holy shit, Kitty Kat." He sighs contentedly. I grin and rest my head on his shoulder, my fingers absently fiddling with his chest hair, his warm arms tight around me, and both of us lie there in the blissful bubble we created around us for a while.

Chapter Five

I'm tired by the time I get back to the hotel in Luton. My morning meeting in London had dragged into afternoon. When I open the room door, I hear the shower running and smell Mike's delicious shower gel. I take a deep breath, enjoying the fresh scent before dropping my bag, kicking off my shoes, and stripping off. I creep quietly into the bathroom, unheard by Mike.

He jumps when I pull back the shower curtain and step in to join him under the warm water. He puts his hands up on the wall and allows me the opportunity to run my hands over every inch of his body. I waste no time in rubbing my fingertips over his broad shoulders, placing kisses over the skin that my fingers have touched. I sweep my hand downwards and cup his ass, allowing a soapy finger to slip between his buttocks. Mike groans and his hips move back against my hand.

"Hello, slut." I grin against his back. He turns and envelops me in his arms, capturing my mouth with his for a smouldering kiss. I wrap my arms around his neck and allow myself to melt in against him.

"Long day?" he murmurs against my neck as he nuzzles into it, nibbling on it gently.

"Something like that," I reply.

Mike turns me in his arms so that my back is against his chest. His hands slide over my shoulders and he starts kneading my flesh firmly. I moan in relaxation as he continues to massage my shoulders. I let my hands slip behind me and find his hard cock. I massage him as he massages me.

His mouth makes contact with my left shoulder, and he bites into my skin. I let my head fall to the side, allowing him more access, enjoying the pleasure the pressure of his mouth is stirring in me. I might like to be dominant, but I enjoy it even more when my possessive alpha marks me and claims me; I'm starting to quite enjoy being his.

"Kat!" he warns as I continue to stroke his length in my hands. He moves against me, his need taking over. My own need to stay in control also rises, and I turn to face him.

"On your knees," I tell him. Mike doesn't argue and sinks to his knees in the bottom of the bathtub. I put a foot up on the side of the bath, opening my legs and exposing my pussy to him.

"What are you waiting for?" I ask. Mike grins as he looks up at me, his mouth inching towards my waiting cunt. His tongue laps from my pussy entrance to my clit. I hiss, fisting one hand in his hair, using the other to steady myself against the cool tiled wall.

He slides his hand up my leg from my calf to my thigh and onwards until he reaches my wet sex. His tongue slips along my entrance, parting my labia for his fingers to slip inside. He fucks into me and wraps his lips around my clit again. He works me until I'm on the edge of orgasm. He nips at my clit with his teeth and a climax slams through me like a tidal wave. I shake against Mike's mouth, my legs barely able to keep me up. His hand slips from me and cups my ass with his other, holding me, making sure that my legs don't buckle.

I need to feel him inside me properly; I don't even need to say it. Mike reads the expression on my face and rises to his feet. His lips meet mine again, and he pulls my leg from the side of the bath to hook it around his hip.

He rubs the tip of his cock against my cunt until it finds its home, and he sinks deep inside me in one movement. My head falls back in ecstasy at the sensation of being filled by him so completely. Mike grabs my hips, pulling me tight against him. He then pulls back before fucking me hard.

I wrap my arms around his neck and hold on to him as he begins to pound into me mercilessly. Mike thrusts hard and my back makes contact with the cold tiles. I hiss. He grins and thrusts into me again, forcing me to make contact with the cold wall for a second time.

I run my hands through his hair and pull. "You'll pay for that," I warn, and he growls with another forceful thrust deep inside me. A moan escapes me on the next stroke, and he picks up the pace a little, pushing me for more moans of pleasure to fall from my lips. I involuntarily give him what he's seeking. My cries grow louder and more frequent. He's pushing me towards another orgasm, and I need it.

Quickly, the waves of pleasure take over, my pussy clamps tightly around his cock, and I climax hard. Mike pauses in his thrusts and waits for my orgasm to wane before he goes straight back to thrusting as deep as he had been, his fingers digging into my buttocks as he keeps me needy.

Mike pushes me to two more orgasms before he thrusts into me so deeply that we bump back, resting against the cold tiles again as he fills me with his cum, deep in my cunt, both of us coming hard. When we both recover, his semi-hard cock slips from my soaked sex. I protest at the absence of him. I move off the tiles and press myself against him, manoeuvring myself back under the warm water.

Mike smiles at me, letting me warm my skin.

"Don't you grin at me, slut," I warn him. "Knees now!"

His cock bobs, coming back to life already as he sinks to his knees. I move forward, place a leg back on the side of the bath, and again expose my pussy to him. He instantly leans in, his tongue slipping once again between my labia.

He moans in appreciation. "Your pussy tastes so good full of my cum," he tells me before plunging his tongue back inside me. I let him; I can never get enough of his mouth on me, his hands on me, his cock inside me. He laps greedily, enjoying the mix of his taste and mine from my cunt.

I grab his hair and pull him back off me. We had talked about some of the things he had secretly fantasised about, and I am just about to indulge him with one of them.

"Open your mouth wide," I command. He does as he's told, and using my grip on his hair, I direct him back close to my pussy. I push, and a warm golden stream starts to flow from my pussy. For a second, he jumps back, but the grip I have on his hair doesn't let him move far. A second more and he moves closer, making sure he catches all of the piss flowing from me.

"That's right. Drink it," I command. "Prove what a filthy little boy you are."

I feel his tongue against me again as I continue to empty my bladder over him. His throat convulses, and I know he's drinking everything I'm giving him.

"Close your mouth," I tell him, and the last of my golden flow hits his closed mouth, runs down over his jaw, his neck, and covers his chest, running down over his rock-hard cock.

When my bladder is finally empty, I tug on his hair again. "Tongue," I demand. His tongue comes out from his mouth, and I wipe myself against it, using him to lick me clean. Once I'm satisfied, I pull him back from my cunt, grab a squirt of shower gel and give myself a wash and rinse off, then I step out of the shower, wrapping a towel around me.

"Clean yourself up, you worthless little piss whore. And don't you dare have a wank," I tell him, fastening the towel at my breasts and leaving him in the bathroom to get cleaned up.

Chapter Six

He wanted me to push him further. He wanted to be even more of a little slut for me, but as he stands in front of me now, dressed up completely in feminine things, I can't help but wonder if I have pushed too hard. I look him up and down as he stands here in stockings, suspenders, knickers, bra, a slutty, club-wear-style revealing red dress, and thigh-high PVC hooker boots. When my gaze meets his, I'm struck by the dangerous look of lust veiled in his hooded lids.

I move towards him and back him up against the wall, grinning at the look on his face, and run my hands over his thighs, up under his skirt. I reach inside his knickers and run my hand over the top of his hard dick, finding it slick with precum already.

"You're so wet for me, my little whore," I tease him and crush my mouth against his, needing to taste him with urgency. His arms instantly tighten around me, pulling me tight against him. I wrap my arms around his neck and deepen our kiss, penetrating his mouth forcefully, loving how his broad, manly frame feels against mine covered in lace and sheer fabrics.

Mike runs his hands along my arms until he reaches my hands, then he circles my wrists with his long fingers. He pulls my hands from behind his head and draws them back behind me, forcing my breasts to stick out proudly, pressing harder against his chest.

I part my lips from his for a moment, ready to complain about him restraining my hands, but he distracts me by nuzzling and nibbling on the sweet spot on my neck before I get the chance. I moan at the delicious sensations his mouth on my neck generates, the tension in my reaction ebbing, replaced by need.

Mike manoeuvres us, his mouth alternating between deep, penetrating kisses to harder and harder nips and kisses on my neck and shoulder. He releases my hands and yanks my dress quickly over my head, undoing my bra and sliding it down my arms.

Once I'm standing in just my knickers, he pulls my hands back behind me and fastens them there with my bra.

"What are you doing?" I ask him in alarm. His finger covers my lips to tell me to stay silent, and he turns me so my back is against his chest. His mouth returns to my shoulder, kissing and nipping at my flesh. His hands, now free from their task of restraining me, move to my breasts. Mike cups my tits firmly in both hands and kneads my flesh, his forefingers and thumbs finding my already hard nipples and rolling them between his digits.

This goes against everything I usually do in play. It ruins the sense of control I like to maintain, and yet because it's Mike, and because of the trust I have in him, the need I have for more of him in this moment far outweighs any need I have to control this situation. He presses his erection against my bound hands as he nuzzles my neck and gropes my tits, and I indulge in a little groping of my own. I wrap my hands around his cock as best I can and move them up and down his length.

Mike groans, and my efforts are rewarded with a harsh bite on my shoulder and a cruel twist of my nipples.

"Ah! Ah!" he warns. "You've been teasing me long enough, Kitty Kat. It's payback time," he announces in a breathless whisper against my ear. A shiver runs through me. The feeling of his hot breath over my skin makes me need him even more than I already do. He moves away from behind me and turns me to face him. "Turn around," he demands, and I find myself willingly turning to face him. "Kneel for me, little Kat," he says softly and kisses the tip of my nose, and I sink to my knees in front of him. The expression on his face when he looks down at me tells me everything I need to know. I know what he's thinking, what he expects from me, and just how turned on he is by the prospect.

He hitches up the hem of his dress, pulls down the front of his lacy panties, and lets his cock spring free at me. Instinctively, I lick and bite at my lips and look up at him. Mike uses his thumb to push down on the length of his cock and point it directly to my mouth.

"Suck it," he tells me.

I open my mouth and take him inside, instantly tasting his precum on my tongue. I moan around the head of his cock as I greedily lap at him. Mike fists his hand in my hair and pushes my mouth down on him further.

I run my tongue over the underside of his length and look up at him. A low groan escapes him and spurs me on. I push further, taking even more of him between my wet lips. Mike's hips twitch, and his grip on my hair tightens.

"You keep looking at me like that, Kitty Kat, and I'll not be able to stop myself from fucking that beautiful face of yours," he warns me breathlessly.

His words fan the flames of my desire. I want him, no I *need* him to push me; I want him to take over. I widen my mouth and push him as far in as my gag reflex allows, holding still when I find my limit and breathing through my nose until it passes.

"Jesus!" he hisses. Unable to resist anymore, Mike pulls back and thrusts into my mouth. He groans a low rumble as he sets a fast pace of claiming my mouth, pushing further and further towards my throat.

My knickers are soaked, and my nipples are painfully hard. I need more of this than I ever imagined possible. It's not until my eyes are wet from fighting the need to gag that Mike pulls his rock-hard and swollen cock from my lips.

"Enough! Get up," he groans and helps to pull me back to my feet. He leads me to the bed and tells me to get my knees onto the bed and move forward. Once he is happy with where I am, he gives me a shove and I fall flat on my face. An instant later, he's between my legs, pushing them further apart, exposing me to him.

He yanks the crotch of my knickers roughly out of the way and sinks into my drenched cunt in one hard stroke. I moan loudly at his abrupt penetration, my voice croaky from the abuse my throat has just taken. Mike begins fucking me with ruthless precision. He pulls out almost completely before forcing himself back in even deeper. It isn't long until my pussy starts to tighten, and that feeling of impending orgasm creeps low in my stomach. Seconds later, on another deep hard thrust, I cry out as an incredible climax consumes me.

As my greedy little cunt pauses in its tight grip on

Mike's dick, he continues his routine of almost withdrawing, followed by a deep hard thrust. My hips instinctively lift against his movements as best they can with my arms behind my back. A second and third orgasm slam into me in quick succession, and suddenly, Mike pulls out.

Before I have the time to protest, his fingers find my juices and start rubbing them up towards my arsehole, making it just as slick as the rest of me. The head of Mike's cock pushes against my ass. I catch my breath as I try to relax, already sure of what's coming next.

Mike puts his weight into pushing into my arse, and after a moment of pressure, he penetrates me once again. I cry out at the sensation, the feeling scorching every nerve ending in my body and sizzling right through to my clit. He's slow and gentle in his movements, but he's taken me so utterly that I'm on a complete overload of sensations. I feel completely possessed by Mike, lying here face down on the bed, my arms tied behind me, and my ass being stretched and filled so deliciously. My little bubble is burst when he leans against me and breathes across my ear.

"What do you call me, Kat?" he whispers.

It takes me a few moments to register what he's asking me while he's pushing deeper into my ass with every stroke.

"What do you call me?" he asks a little more loudly.

"A whore," I answer with a moan as he thrusts back into me slowly.

"And if you're being fucked in the arse by the whore, what does that make you?"

I groan at where this conversation is going. I know what he's doing. It's the game I've played on him. It's the words and the taunting I've done. I just never realised how potent they were on the receiving end.

"What am I, Kat?" he insists, the pace of his thrusts picking up.

"A whore," I moan.

"What does that make you?" he asks again.

"The whore's whore," I cry out as another orgasm starts to wash over me.

"Fuck." The almost plea-like outburst comes from behind me as my body clenches and releases with the climax.

A soft sheen of sweat has settled over my body. I feel wrung out, and yet so in need of even more from Mike. As my senses clear a little, he picks up the pace.

"You have a whore in a dress deep in your ass, Kitty Kat," he teases me breathlessly.

A groan rumbles through me; I'm turned on like I've never been before, and this man is the reason. This experience is fast becoming the most liberating thing I've ever done. His breathing hitches, and I feel him pulse in my ass. I know just how close he is. I can feel another climax building in me, and I'm overcome with the urgency to have him join me.

"Oh, fuck," I moan. "Fill me. Make me your whore."

My words become both our undoing; he bucks against my ass in one hard movement, a guttural moan resonating through him. I clamp around him and cry out as I come once more. Mike jerks inside me as he comes hard, deep in my ass. Moments pass as we both recover from the shattering climaxes that have quaked through us.

He pulls his semi-erect cock slowly from my arse and drops down onto the bed beside me. His hand goes to my wrists, and my bra is untied, freeing me from my binds. I grumble as the stiffness in my shoulders becomes apparent, moving against Mike to be on my side against him. My hand comes down over his chest and I rub my fingers lazily over his chest hair. When I glance up at him, his lips come down hard on mine.

"Thank you," he murmurs against my lips.

"What for?" I ask him.

"Your trust," he replies. "And you have no idea how sexy it is to think of my cum deep inside you." He grins and possesses my mouth once more. I surrender to him, silently acknowledging the trust I have in him, and how right he is about being claimed.

Chapter Seven

Mike has been teasing me with some sort of surprise for the entire fortnight that he had to be in the States for business. He had told me a few days ago; it was something he'd had since just before he left.

He walks in, scoops me up, and kisses me hard. "I have fucking missed you!" he murmurs against my neck, peppering it with kisses. "I need to be inside you, Kitty Kat."

I can't help but agree with the way he's thinking. It's been too long. I missed him. I missed how his hands feel on my naked skin, and how his mouth feels on mine, and most importantly, how perfectly he fits inside me to rock me to climax.

I smile and nuzzle into his chest. "I thought you had something for me," I say with a grin.

Mike flashes a grin back, and with a raised eyebrow, replies, "Oh, you know I do!" He flexes his hip against me so I feel his hard cock through his jeans.

I roll my eyes. "That wasn't what I meant, and you

know it. But I'll take it!" I say, grabbing his hand and pulling him upstairs behind me.

Mike wastes no time in pulling me against him again when we reach my bedroom. He surrounds me in his arms, plants his lips on mine, and pulls me so tight against him it's almost like he's trying to fuse us together.

He grabs the hem of my t-shirt, tugging it over my head and throwing it across the room. I go for his shirt, and he pulls away from me, holding up a finger, silently telling me to wait. He kicks off his shoes, removes his socks, and looks at me through hooded eyelids.

"Strip for me," he says, his eyes roaming over my already exposed flesh. I turn my back to him and grab the waistband of my leggings, peeling them down over my ass, revealing a lacy little red thong. When my leggings reach the floor, I kick them to the side. I turn back to face him and undo my bra, letting my breasts spill from the cups as it slides down my arms. I throw that to the side, and it lands with my discarded leggings. I let my hands skim over my breasts, dropping them to my sides; I'm purposely not taking off my knickers yet. Not until he's lost more of his clothing.

"Now what?" I ask innocently.

Mike's primal look almost sets me on fire with the intensity of his gaze. "Oh, you'll lose those soon enough," he warns with a devilish glint in his eyes.

I take his unspoken challenge and move towards him. I grab the waist of his jeans and unbutton them. I then pull down the zipper and hook my thumbs in, sliding Mike's boxers and jeans down. He steps out of them, and I bend to move them out of the way. His cock bobs beside my head, and I look up at him, never breaking eye contact as I wrap my lips around the head of his cock and take him deep into my mouth.

A loud gasp comes from Mike as I suck on his length. "Fuck!" he hisses. His hand naturally goes to the back of my head. He sighs in satisfaction when he is able to push me and sink further into my mouth.

When he finds my gag point, he groans and pulls out of my mouth with a pop. "I have to have you," he says, and I move to undo the buttons of his shirt before running my hands underneath and pushing it off his shoulders and down his arms.

I'm about to lean in to kiss him again when something on his chest catches my eye. On his left pec, under a tuft of chest hair that's barely there compared to the rest, is a tattoo. In a little black outline, looking almost sexy, is a cat. Underneath it in a delicate script is, "My Kitty Kat."

I stare at it, lifting my fingers over it without actually making contact.

"Do you like it?" he asks anxiously.

I look up at him. "You have my name on your skin forever?"

"Unless you really piss me off, and I go for laser removal." He grins.

I'm astounded at the gesture he's made; he's left me lost for words for a change.

"Do you like it?" he asks, his arms around me again.

"Yes." I say, trying not to overthink the 'what ifs.' "I love it," I admit.

"You're so fond of marking me, Kitten, I thought I'd make it permanent."

My lips crash into his and I claim his mouth. I'm moved by his actions, unable to express myself, so I show him how I feel. He pulls me hard against him, amplifying my passion with his own. His hands slide down my sides and he rips my thong off, pulling it from my body in tattered pieces. He lifts me, and I hook my legs around his hips, and my arms around his neck. He sinks me down on his cock until he is fully sheathed in my wet cunt.

He thrusts into me slowly and I start to feel overwhelmed by the sensations and the emotions of the moment. I find myself needy and feeling emotionally raw. When Mike thrusts in deep, words unexpectedly fall from my lips on a sigh.

"Fuck, I love you," I breathe. I don't get the chance to overthink what I've just uttered. Mike's thrusts pick up the pace and I'm lost to the sensations he's generating within me.

"I feel just the same about you. Move in with me," he pants, pausing his thrusts. I move against him, and he holds me still. "Move in with me," he murmurs against my lips. Again, I try to get the friction I need, and he holds me tighter still. "Kat," he growls.

"This is sexual blackmail!" I glare at him.

"I love you. Move in with me," he says again.

"Fine," I agree, desperate to feel him moving against me.

"Yes?" he asks.

"Yes! Okay, yes!" I exclaim.

We land on the bed a moment later, and he begins thrusting into me again, racing me to the climax I have been so desperate for.

—

A few weeks later, after talking it all over, Mike brings his stuff over and he moves into my house with me. Things are still evolving. I enjoy the control as much as I ever did. But I'm also learning that the take part can be just as much fun as the give.

THE END.

* * *

Enjoy this? Why not read the next in the series - Tempted

What if you had just one night?

Gemma is happily married, faithful, successful business. Everything she thought she wanted.

Noah is a happy, successful, ex serviceman. But he's never forgotten his first love. The one that got away.

A chance meeting in a hotel miles from home throws them back into each others' paths. What would you do if fate gave you a chance to see what you had missed out on all those years ago? Would you resist, or would you be tempted.

About the Author

Dee Lish is an Irish author who loves to indulge her imagination with some filthy stories. She's been publishing under other pen names since 2014, but in 2023 returned to her erotic roots.

She likes to spend what little spare time she has binge watching her favourite shows, reading, and making messes and memories with her two children.

You can follow her on social media, or join her newsletter for all the latest naughtiness!

Also by Dee Lish

Succumb to Me Series

The Mistress

The Ponygirl

The Handled

The Punished

The Corrupted

The Student

One Handed Reads Series

Teased

Owned

Seduced

Tempted

Desired

Unexpected

* * *

Dee Lish also writes romance as Leighann Duncan

www.authorleighannduncan.co.uk

www.ingramcontent.com/pod-product-compliance
Lightning Source LLC
Chambersburg PA
CBHW030810190726
48285CB00003B/1117